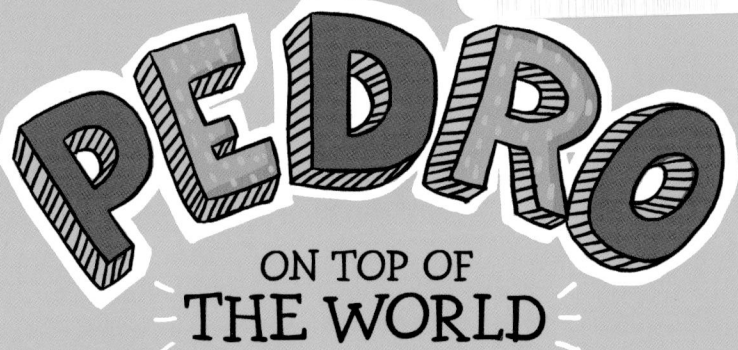

PEDRO

ON TOP OF
THE WORLD

by Fran Manushkin

illustrated by
Tammie Lyon

Pedro is published by Picture Window Books,
a Capstone Imprint
1710 Roe Crest Drive
North Mankato, Minnesota 56003
www.mycapstone.com

Text ©2019 Fran Manushkin
Illustrations ©2019 Picture Window Books

Cataloging-in-Publication Data is available on the Library of Congress website.
ISBN: 978-1-5158-2823-5 (library binding)
ISBN: 978-1-5158-2828-0 (paperback)
ISBN: 978-1-5158-2839-6 (eBook pdf)

Summary: Pedro's family is spending the day with their friends at an amusement park. Everyone is having a wonderful time until Pedro's brother, Paco, gets lost! Can a ride on the Ferris wheel lead Pedro back to Paco?

Designer: Kayla Rossow
Design Elements by Shutterstock

Printed and bound in the USA.
PA021

Table of Contents

Chapter 1
Family Fun Park

"Yay!" yelled Pedro. "We are finally at Family Fun Park. Let's stay all day. It's great at night too."

Pedro, Katie, and JoJo loved
riding the Tilt-and-Twirl.

"Spin faster!" yelled Pedro.

"I'm dizzy!" yelled Katie.

"I'm not," said Pedro.

Then they rode the Rapid

River Flume. The ride was

fierce and fast.

"That was fun," said Pedro.

"But I want a scary ride."

"Here's a wild ride," said
Pedro's dad. "Let's try the
Ferris Wheel."

Pedro watched the big
wheel spinning, rising high
into the sky. "Hmm," he said.
"Maybe later."

Chapter 2

Where's Paco?

"I want cotton candy!"

yelled Pedro's brother, Paco.

"I see popcorn!" said Pedro.

"Can we get some?"

Pedro's mom took Paco to get cotton candy. Pedro and his dad walked the other way to get popcorn.

The line for popcorn was very long. It took a while to get some.

"Now," said Pedro's dad, "let's go back to your mom and the others."

They found Katie and

JoJo eating ice cream with

Katie's mom.

"Have you seen my mom

and Paco?" asked Pedro.

"No," said Katie.

Pedro and his dad searched and searched. Finally, they found Pedro's mom. She was searching too!

"A parade came by," she said, "and Paco got lost in the crowd."

"I'll tell the lost and found," said Katie's mom.

"The rest of us will keep searching," said Pedro's dad. "We have to hurry. It will be dark soon."

Chapter 3
Be Brave, Pedro!

"I have an idea!" said

Pedro's dad. "Let's take a ride

on the Ferris Wheel. From high

up, we can see the whole park.

It's a fast way to find Paco."

"I can't," said Pedro. "It's too scary!"

Pedro began walking away. But then he came back. "My brother is in trouble!" he said. "I have to be brave."

When the wheel began spinning, Pedro held his dad's hand. Up went the big wheel, higher and higher and *HIGHER*!

At the top, it stopped!

"Yikes!" yelled Pedro's dad.

"I'm not wild about this."

He closed his eyes. But

Pedro kept his eyes open.

There was so much to see!

"Dad," Pedro yelled, "open your eyes! This is *fun,* and I can see Paco!"

"Wow!" Pedro's dad smiled. "This is awesome!"

After a few more spins,
Pedro and his dad were back
on the ground. Pedro led his
dad to Paco.

Oh, was there hugging!

"I was in a parade!" bragged Paco. "This park is fun!"

"Sometimes," said his dad.

"Always!" yelled Pedro. "I was brave. *Boy*, was I brave!"

Soon everyone was back together.

"Before we go," said Katie, "let's ride the Cannonball Roller Coaster."

"Yikes!" said Pedro's mom.

"That's high—and FAST."

"Don't worry," said Pedro's

dad. "If you take Pedro, he

will help you be brave."

And he did!

About the Author

Fran Manushkin is the author of many popular picture books, including *Happy in Our Skin; Baby, Come Out!; Latkes and Applesauce: A Hanukkah Story; The Tushy Book; Big Girl Panties; Big Boy Underpants;* and *Bamboo for Me, Bamboo for You!* There is a real Katie Woo—she's Fran's great-niece—but she never gets in half the trouble of the Katie Woo in the books. Fran writes on her beloved Mac computer in New York City, without the help of her two naughty cats, Chaim and Goldy.

About the Illustrator

Tammie Lyon began her love for drawing at a young age while sitting at the kitchen table with her dad. She continued her love of art and eventually attended the Columbus College of Art and Design, where she earned a bachelor's degree in fine art. After a brief career as a professional ballet dancer, she decided to devote herself full time to illustration. Today she lives with her husband, Lee, in Cincinnati, Ohio. Her dogs, Gus and Dudley, keep her company as she works in her studio.

Glossary

awesome (AW-suhm)—causing a feeling of admiration or wonder

crowded (KROW-did)—filled with too many people or things

Ferris Wheel (FAYR-is WEEL)—a very large wheel that has seats where people sit while the wheel turns; a ride at an amusement park

fierce (FEERSS)—daring and dangerous or strong

lost and found (LOST AND FOUND)—a place where lost children or items are kept until someone comes to claim them

rapid (RA-pid)—very fast or quick

Let's Talk

1. Pedro and the others ride a lot of amusement park rides in the story. Did you ever ride on a roller coaster? What about a Ferris Wheel? Would you like to?

2. What would you do if you were lost in a public place like Paco was? How would you stay safe and be found?

3. At first, Pedro seems afraid to ride the Ferris Wheel, but he remembers he needs to help Paco. Talk about a time that you overcame a fear.

Let's Write

1. Amusement parks have a lot of special foods you can buy. What are your favorite treats or snacks? Make a list.

2. Draw your very own roller coaster or ride! Give it a name and write a few of its special features beside it.

3. Think about what you do when you can't find something you've lost. Then write a guide with numbered steps that tells someone how to find something they've lost.

JOKE AROUND

- What does a dentist do on a roller coaster?
  He braces himself.

- Why didn't the skeleton ride the roller coaster?
  He didn't have the guts.

- Knock, knock
  Who's there?
  Howard
  Howard who?
  Howard you like to go to the amusement park?

- What is a bride and groom's favorite ride?
  the married-go-round

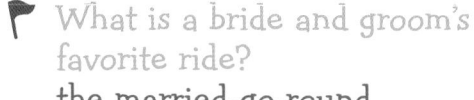

WITH PEDRO!

- Why did the chicken cross the amusement park?
  to get to the other ride

- Why don't mummies go to amusement parks?
  They're afraid to relax and unwind.

- Do fish like to visit amusement parks?
  No, they are always in school!

- What is a frog's favorite treat at the amusement park?
  hopsicles

THE FUN DOESN'T STOP HERE!

Discover more at www.capstonekids.com

- Videos & Contests
- Games & Puzzles
- Friends & Favorites
- Authors & Illustrators

Find cool websites and more books like this one at www.facthound.com. Just type in the Book ID: 9781515828235 and you're ready to go!

31901063483467

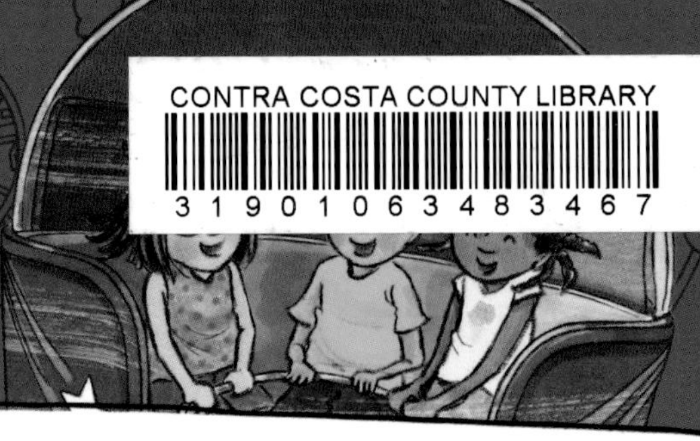

From the creators
of Katie Woo comes Pedro,

A BOY WITH BIG PLANS
TO HAVE BIG FUN!

Pedro's family is spending the day with
their friends at an amusement park.
Everyone is having a wonderful time until
Pedro's brother, Paco, gets lost! Can a ride on
the Ferris Wheel lead Pedro back to Paco?

capstone
www.mycapstone.com

F&P Text Level Gradient™
Officially Leveled by **Fountas & Pinnell**

9 781515 828280